Sheila Wolk ©

I am so excited to bring you my first ever Sheila Wolk Coloring Books.

I grew up creating and coloring my own coloring books from childhood to teen and now as an adult I bring my coloring pages of my original paintings for you to color, relax and enjoy using colored pencils, markers, gel pens and more.

My art career has spanned over 50 years as a world renowned artist in Sports to Ballet, Entertainment and now Fantasy Art.

HINT: This coloring book is not suitable for any water mediums or markers unless you put a piece of card stock or a few pieces of regular paper between the pages to prevent bleeding through.

May my fantasy art adult coloring books bring you relaxing fun art therapy as my paintings have done for me for 50 years.

May you have as much fun coloring these pages as I do in creating my paintings.
You can see what my paintings and colors look like in my websites at:
www.sheilawolkart.com   or   www.sheilawollk.com

"without fantasy, there is no dream"

This book was
colored by
and belongs to:

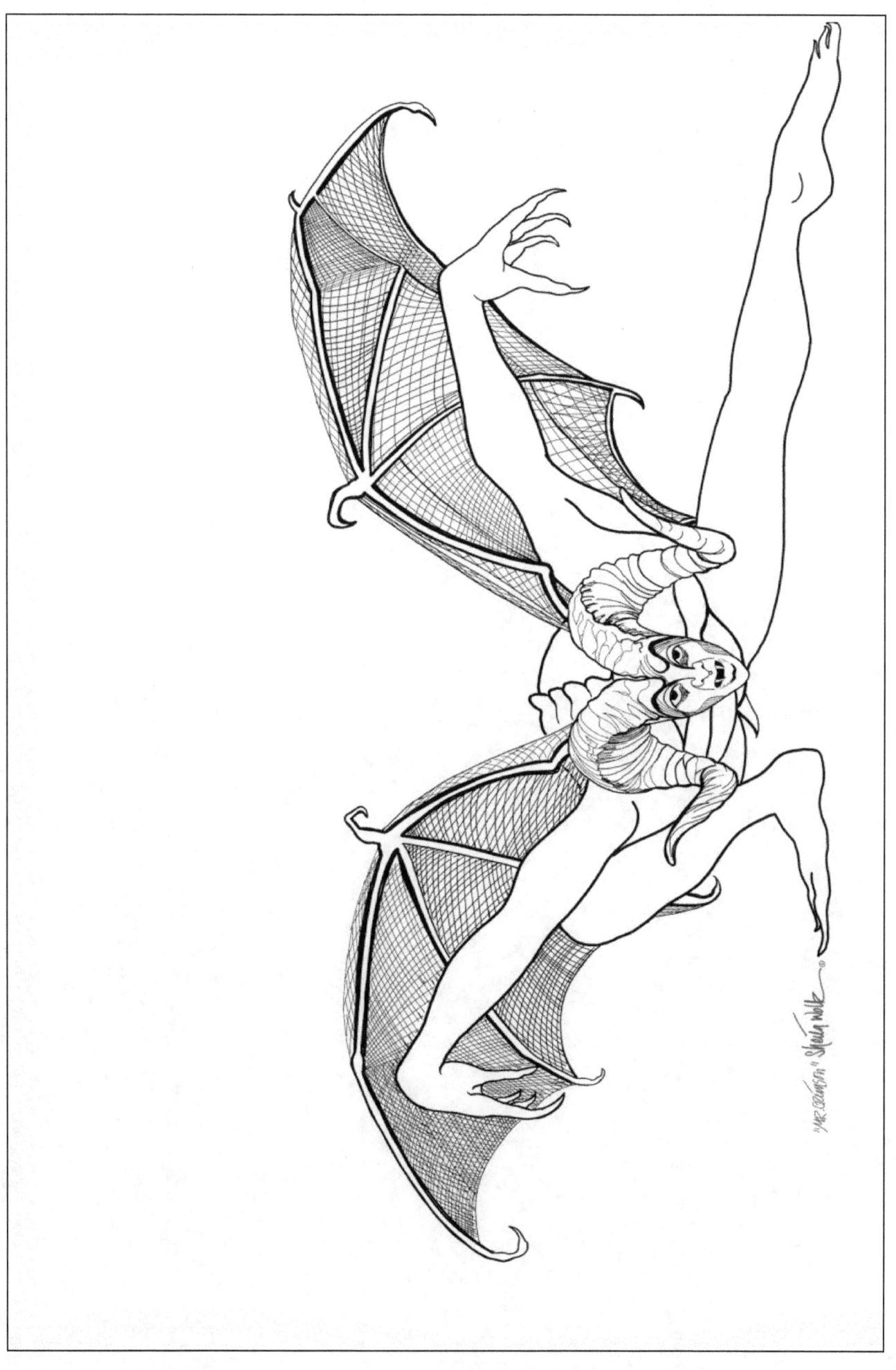

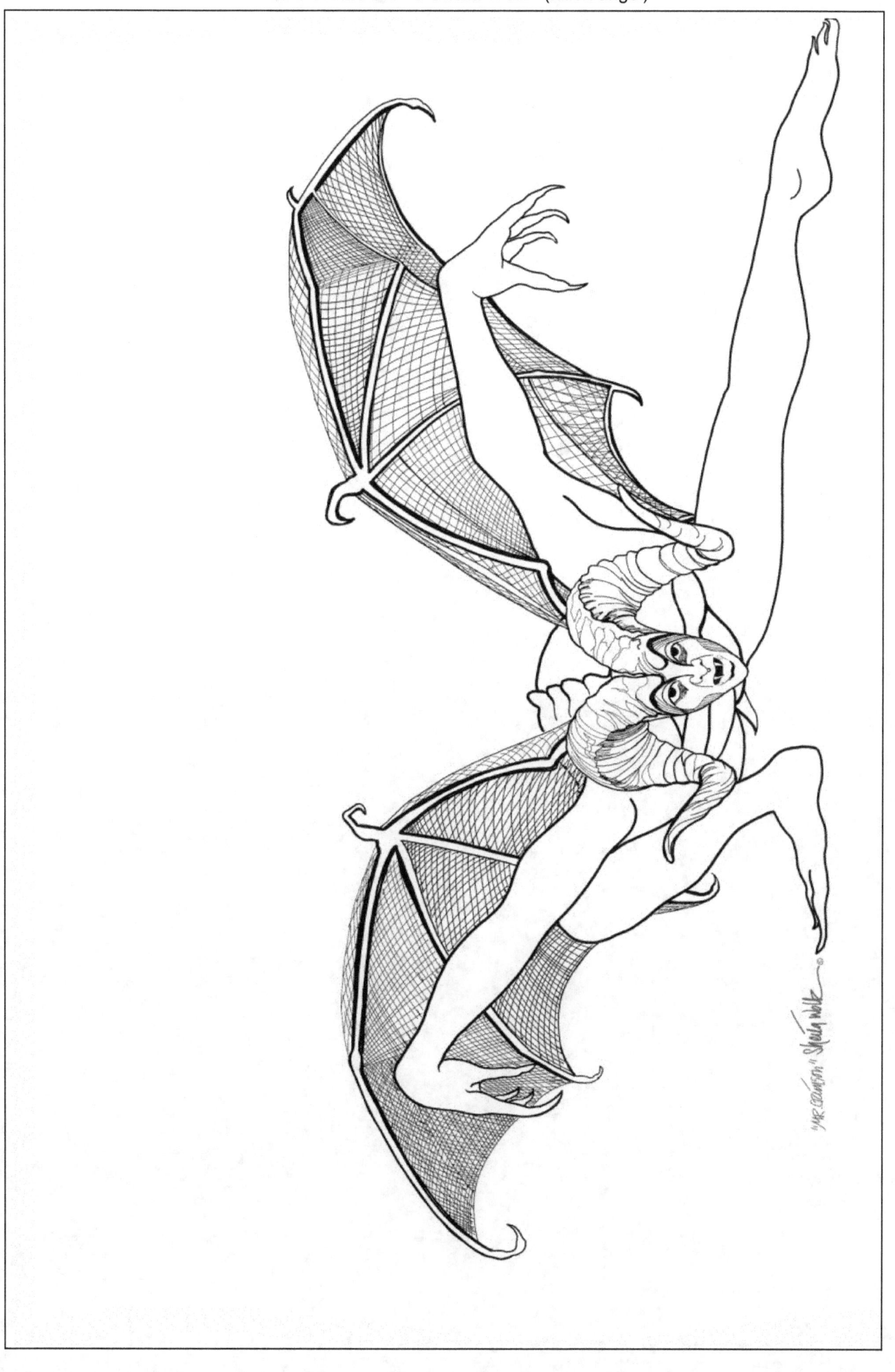

www.ingramcontent.com/pod-product-compliance
Lightning Source LLC
Chambersburg PA
CBHW081147170626
46809CB00010B/3124